THE PUP GREW UP!

THE PUP GREW UP!
WRITTEN BY **SAMUEL MARSHAK**
TRANSLATED FROM THE RUSSIAN BY **RICHARD PEVEAR**
ILLUSTRATED BY **VLADIMIR RADUNSKY**

HENRY HOLT AND COMPANY  NEW YORK

Translation copyright © 1989 by Richard Pevear
Illustrations copyright © 1989 by Vladimir Radunsky
All rights reserved, including the right to reproduce this book or
portions thereof in any form.
Published by Henry Holt and Company, Inc., 115 West 18th Street, New
York, New York 10011.
Published in Canada by Fitzhenry & Whiteside Limited, 195 Allstate
Parkway, Markham, Ontario L3R 4T8.

Library of Congress Cataloging-in-Publication Data
Marshak, S. (Samuel), 1887–1964.
    The pup grew up! / by Samuel Marshak ; translated by Richard
Pevear ; illustrated by Vladimir Radunsky.
    Translated from Russian.
    Summary: A comic poem in which a woman who is traveling by train
finds that her Pekingese puppy is missing and has been replaced by
a Great Dane.
    ISBN 0-8050-0952-3
    [1. Dogs—Fiction.   2. Railroads—Fiction.   3. Stories in rhyme.]
I. Pevear, Richard.   II. Radunsky, Vladimir, ill.   III. Title.
PZ8.3.M394Pu   1989   [E]—dc19   88-28428
Henry Holt books are available at special discounts for bulk purchases
for sales promotions, premiums, fund-raising, or educational use.
Special editions or book excerpts can also be created to specification.

For details, contact: Special Sales Director, Henry Holt & Co., Inc., 115
West 18th Street, New York, New York 10011.

Designed by Vladimir Radunsky

Printed in Hong Kong
10 9 8 7 6 5 4 3 2 1

Samuel Marshak was the best-loved
children's book author in the Soviet Union.
He organized the first publishing house for
children's books and played a leading role
in shaping Soviet literature for children. He
also created the first children's theater and
the first children's literary magazine.

Marshak's best-known stories and
poetry for children were written and
published in the late twenties and early
thirties. *The Postman* and *The Ice Cream
Man and Other Stories* were published in
this country in 1943.

Marshak translated into Russian the
sonnets of Shakespeare and the poetry of
Byron and Robert Burns and in many other
ways helped bridge the gap between
Soviet and Western literature.

Samuel Marshak was born in Voronezh,
Russia, in 1887, and died in Moscow
in 1964.

A lady came to the station
  With a pan
  A divan
  A basin
  A box
  With three locks
  A valise
And a tiny Pekingese.

REGISTRATION

She insisted at the station
On the proper registration
    Of her pan
    Her divan
    Her basin
    Her box
    With three locks
    Her valise
And her tiny Pekingese.

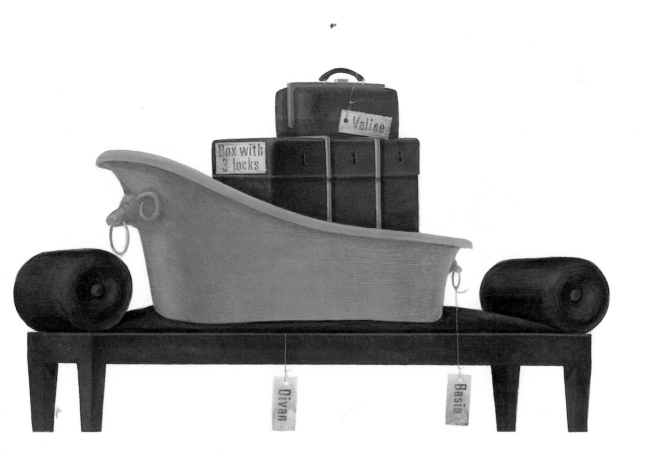

The redcap puffed a cigar
As he loaded the baggage car.

All aboard! We're off on vacation
    With a pan
    A divan
    A basin
    A box
    With three locks
    A valise
And a tiny Pekingese!

But when the platform was bare,
The puppy was still there.

The train arrived at Gissing
With one piece of baggage missing.
They counted in frustration
  One pan
  One divan
  One basin
  One box
  With three locks
  One valise...
Hey, boys, where's the Pekingese?

They happened to see a Great Dane
Sniffing around the train.
They caught him without hesitation
And put him aboard with the basin
    The pan and the divan
    The box
    With three locks
    The valise—
In place of the Pekingese.

When they came to Bowling Green,
Redcap number 15
Unloaded at their destination
    The pan
    The divan
    The basin
    The box
    With three locks
    The valise
And the dog, last but not least.

The dog began to growl,
The lady began to howl:
"Thieves! Robbers! Hold the train!
This beast is a Great Dane!"

And she gave a swift kick to the pan
And knocked aside the divan
    The box
    With three locks
    The valise...

"Where is my Pekingese???!"

"Excuse me, ma'am, the slip
   They wrote at the start of your trip
   Says you checked into the station
      With...

A pan
A divan
A basin
A box
With three locks
A valise
And a tiny Pekingese

"Maybe
During the trip
Your little pup
Grew up!"

London
To
Bowling Green

No.   First Class, 1^S   6^D

6 day of *A* 192*7*

Please to hold this Ticket till called for.